Sava

Alexis V

The moral right of the author has been asserted. All characters in this publication are fictitious and any resemblance to real persons, living or dead is purely coincidental. It bears no legitimacy to the actual world or any person or organization in it. Cover design by Peter Vincent.

--ISBN: 9798662996946--

Contents

Dedication

To All People of All Races

who deserve inner peace, love and identity

Acknowledgement

Appreciation, much love and gratitude go to my husband Peter who always engages with my ideas and enables me by providing infinite support, in whatever my limitless pursuits require. With boundless patience he accedes to all my design requests as he continues to be my book cover designer and illustrator. Thanks also go to God for continuing to grant me a creative mind.

Prologue

Out of despair some measure of good should result and this book was first written in 2019 when Hurricane Dorian one of the strongest hurricanes on record struck the islands of the Bahamas. With deep sadness, my husband and I watched the news, sympathized and talked about the unfortunate and devastating carnage inflicted on the people of the islands.

During our conversation, it became apparent that the destruction was quite symbolic to what results from the action and process of the unjust or prejudicial treatment of different groups of people. Consequently, this story was formed. It seeks to get the reader, irrespective of race, involved in a conscious and honest self-appraisal of their views on their attitudes and thoughts towards others.

Episode One

Alaric's eyes dimmed as a dark grin creased his lips. This was the time, the season, the exact and precise circumstance which his mind had long ago imagined. He had waited years for this time to come, a brutal storm, a fierce hurricane which would calm his heart.

He had prayed for so long for God to send these hurricane gale force winds which would act as an abundant mask, enough to cover their tracks. He and his sister Diara felt confident that all the debris of this violent storm would wash away any trail of their path. It would remove their scents from this broken earth. They readied themselves, hatchet, machete all sharpened with edges glistening as their eyes perceived the precision strikes and the delight of avenging all the past wrongs.

How many times, how many places, where these two were called carbon-copies, negatives, double AA dead batteries, milky Angus, missing pigments, half-breed? Yes, how many times? Alaric recalled as he quickly glanced at Diara. She too had the same thoughts running wild within her brain.

They had lived a thousand lives within their young years, moved from pillar to post. The twin product of parents who had only desired the best in life for them but had failed in understanding the world and its twisted values.

Alaric shook his long plaits from off his forehead as violent gusts ripped at his flimsy clothing which were it seemed, designed for nothing more than their purpose, as garments of a judge and executioner. His tall imposing figure, yellowish skin, reigned back from the bitter squalls. He and his sister both stood in the doorway of the ramshackle place which they called home. It appeared ready to cave in, crumbling, carelessly and roughly constructed, a rundown shack. This was the island paradise which their parents had promised.

Years before they were told that they were to live with 'gran, gran' on a sun-filled island away from the torture of the western world. Their parents had said, 'you two will be treated well, people will accept you and most of all you will be able to make friends and fit in!'

Was it planned deception to end the punishment for themselves as parents of mixed-race semi-albino twins? Diara inwardly questioned or was it a naïve view of island perceptions? Whatever the misguided intention, she and her brother got plummeted like ackees falling to the ground, then deliberately stepped on bursting out from the seeds. Diara looked at Alaric, he shook his head. He too knew, that this place was really hell!

The wild wind was lashing so viciously about Diara's face she could barely see as they rushed out of the doorway. There were no vehicles and no people; the trees creaked, screaming as their limbs trashed about against nature's torturous onslaught.

Alaric took a few strained steps backwards and scrambled to clutch on to Diara's arm. Lightning struck and sliced the sky while thunder roared in blaring booms! The machete slipped from Alaric's grip as the rain bashed his skin making it raw in seconds. The two rushed on against the blast as they treaded, the wind cut into them as if they were naked but they refused to cringe. They turned a corner and quickened their steps, their faces stung and their eyes narrowed to keep out the relentless veil of rain and the scorching thoughts of sorrows past. They refused to be diminished by this storm, they welcome it as their brother in arms, a kind-hearted donation from the angelic creator. For only such violence as this, can deliver them.

This troubled twin does not fear what is ahead, only what is behind them. The past. Diara felt it had left them without ability, influence, or power to build an existence of substance. She knew that uniqueness was the assets, beliefs, character, looks and expressions that make a person. It correlated with self-image, one's mental prototype of oneself, self-esteem, and individuality. What life model did they have, she silently questioned.

Diara's ankle twisted as she slipped into a large puddle, she glanced down at it. Their lives she thought represented this murky dark hole, with its swirling, swivel of sewage. Alaric tugged on her arm and pulled her out of the hole but she remained glued to her thoughts. This time, this night was the way to get even. They were too far gone; she couldn't give a damn!

It was the time to do what you do, listen to your instincts, listen to what your senses tell you to do. Get primal but don't mess around with doubts. Just make calculating but most of all, deadly moves.

Alaric and her had been close from birth, no one else knew her better and he knew that he could depend on her to take no prisoners and deliver the blows. They would be a force to reckon with, and scared of at all times; this was their convincing alibi. This night, this magnificent night, as this hurricane grew into a whirling behemoth over this island. One hundred and forty kilometre an hour winds lashed the shore, letting these hostile villagers know that this fury was only a taster of what was really in store.

The sounds of laughter which used to fill the air as this twin walked the sandy shores, poking fun at their skin colour was now hushed and an eerie silence occupied the savage wind. The wind was like nothing they had ever heard or seen, violent and unyielding, just plain raw power adding strength to their determination to commit these dark but justifiable deeds. Wanting it to stop was like beseeching a bullet; it was approaching and nothing would stop it.

Running now against the objecting forceful wind, they reached their first prey, Mildred Sizes. Mildred had a bosom which entered any room long before she did and her backside reached her destination many minutes later. She owned a prestigious beach front bar and each swig of the signature cocktail which she served, got worse with taste; until you finally got convinced that it surely had to be whale piss!

Mildred Sizes, ensured that her daughter Wendy, who favoured Alaric clearly understood that to 'mix with' and 'like' Alaric was the biggest sin that could ever be committed. Mildred sharply pointed out, that any relationship with Alaric would certainly devalue their family status and self-worth. Therefore, Mildred 'politely' warned Alaric to keep away since as she put it, 'you could even be charged for us believing that you are thinking about rape, and besides, you coloureds spread a lot of disease!' Her poisonous dwarf mouth continued to spread its venom on him, as she laughed and gossiped about, he and Diara's skin colour and life lot.

Nonetheless, Alaric and Diara had a mental hit list from so long ago, and they both knew that revenge is a hate dish best served cold. This night was ripe as their cold hearts were made icy and frozen not just from the rain but from years of ostracising, ridicule and discrimination; abuse of the mind and destruction of the soul. Many times, they were told by Mildred Sizes, 'animals know their places in life; monkeys never try to mix with lions! You two ought to know that!" These thoughts had constant occupation within their beings.

Reverting to the present, they peeped inside Mildred Sizes' blown opened window as the furious wind crackled and hissed. They inched inside and their eyes darted all around, when suddenly Mildred Sizes', underwear was ripped by the wind from her indoors' washing line! Alaric ducked but was too slow, Mildred Sizes oversized banga Marys acted like sails and hit Alaric right in the face!

Diara swiftly rushed to Alaric's aid, she used all her strength to help him untangle himself from this bloomers' prison stockade! They pulled and tugged with all their might! Several seconds passed and finally, Alaric was freed from Mildred Sizes most definite passion killers. Quickly wiping his face, he and Diara now looked all around but Mildred Sizes was nowhere to be found!

Alaric and Diara's legs backed away and on reaching outside their feet quickly hit the ground. As they ran on, they thought that Mildred Sizes' elusive absence was just like their lives, never achieving what they wanted, always missing out and having to move on. Constantly being rebuffed and hit in the face!

Blistering thoughts now flew through Alaric's head. Oh, he knew so very well, that his personality was defined from the distinctive set of behaviours, reasonings, and emotional patterns that evolved from biological and environmental factors. He roughly wiped his rain drenched face; his feet flew as his thoughts blew on in his brain. He had high education there was no doubt but invariably he got no job. When he was offered work his knowledge was wasted on the menial jobs, he was given which required no skill and those which lacked prestige or even use of engaging intellectual thought. Once on a brief return to Britain, with high hopes, he recalled the only job he got was with a broom. His boss even argued that he left bread crumbs untouched and so his wages would be docked. At the end of his shift in that bakery, he was offered bread which enjoyed having mildew as a close company friend. His boss defended himself and said, the bread was no offense, that he had heard that mildew worked wonders for people like him. He further explained that this was a mere kind gesture, no need to feel insulted.

Alaric now laughed to himself as they stopped and rested back on a railing, panting to catch their breaths. What support did they have to live in the colour of their skin? He wasn't white enough to be accepted by the whites and he wasn't black enough to be truly liked by the blacks. Worse yet, he was fated to be different in a state of having a skin condition which also engendered mocking and even stoked hate.

Everywhere they went it was the same façade, pretence of smiles, polite conversation, just to tolerate what some called them, nondescript human beings. Some would invite you round for a drink, a few minutes spent but only outside in their back yard. 'See that proves that I do mix,' they'd say.

However, while in that yard the conversation would be, 'can you clean up and weed up that garden bed for me?' Could he count on anyone of them as a true friend? And precisely, how many friendships did they have, that were genuine? He asked himself? Mistrust was deep, but skin colour judgement was deeper still. They got endless false actions which they knew were at odds with strong held beliefs. While cruel and harsh treatments erased any mercy seat.

Then again, why blame outsiders, what about family? Were their parents proud of them? They hid them away on this God forsaken island, in hope that they would find their niche. Growing up, their parents had said that in Britain blacks had a powerful ability of making white people vanish. In their neighbourhood, a black person only had to step outside and every white person would quickly disappear inside!

Needless to say, if they had asked any white person, 'how many black people have you ever had round for dinner?' Most certainly, the extreme outraged look on their face, or subtle avoidance, provided the answer of an emphatic shout of, 'for fox sake NONE!' This twin's community engaged more with four-legged friends than it did with non-white humans. The white folks laughed and talked with their pet dogs and cats, and to be sure, this twins' former school was named after a race horse, Laureate the III!

Discrete talk abounded back in Britain, yes, with solutions for everything. They said, 'really it's not your fault that you are not the same, not different, don't say different, don't say not normal either, that's not nice; you're both just not the same.

There is a limit to how much mixing we can do, otherwise we could end up just like you being eschewed and left out from social dos! We never discriminate like in America, oh no! We treat our black servants really well but it just won't look good for you to be at our teas!' These very polite apologetic human excuses for man's inhumanity to man, Alaric and Diara grappled with, and were inscribed under their skin. Itched and hotly burnt in, until the pain gradually became a 'normal' way of life which they had no control over.

Hopeful thought for sanctuary here on this island was very swiftly blown away, with stares, snickers, suppressed laughs and typically scornful glares. It was the same shit, just a different pattern all over again! The far and long reach of skin colour rejection still stuck its tentacles deep into their souls. It was in their conscious existence and wormed its way beneath the subconscious, where there was no escape from its torturous load.

They were told by several counsellors that they had to be motivated to build their lives. That to get a strong character, sound identity was based on having motivation and psychological interactions with one's environment. These highly informed transparent skin colour authorities couldn't find their ass if it was sat on their face.

Alaric and Diara knew that in a world where every environment rejects you, based on skin colour then you must turn to an alternate world. This now, was their new world, one of rightful retribution. They were now highly stirred to connect and engage; there would be no mercy.

Shifting their thoughts back to the present, Alaric and Diara's feet now moved with stealth as the tempestuous gales pushed them along within the rising waters in the streets. They watched as driveways disappeared in the deluge that descended upon this island. They were indebted to this night which was blackened by the power outage and the encompassing wrath of the cloud laden sky. They rounded another corner and here, this would be a serious reckoning with the devils. The one within their souls and the one which inhabited the minds of the populace who saw distinctions between humanity. The one which created labels for humans, partitioned and divided them.

With lightning speed, they now reached old Smiley's house. He had so many lines on his face that hugged each other as testimony to a long life, with a reward of a ripe old age. He really had gone way passed his sell by date. Smiley they knew had the morals of a rabbit; his offspring could be found in almost every local home on the island. Smiley's generation could be excused for its ignorance and reluctance to understand that each individual is unique, and recognizing that our individual differences are wide and varied. In Smiley's time, black was black and white was white, any, 'half caste' or 'ekey becky' as Smiley called them, he didn't want to know about. It was unnatural, and any off spring was cursed.

This brother and sister knew that if a blood test was performed on Smiley, it would be determining how much blood was in Smiley's alcohol. Still, to the locals, Smiley was a respected island figure. He led the charge on perspectives despite his toothless-mouth spouting of all manner of irrelevant shit.

Turning now, they looked at each other, the hatchet and machete were tightly gripped. Smiley's house stared them in the face. Its darkness enveloped and subsumed the bending trees. They crept up to the boarded-up window, then suddenly the door blew open! They held back in absolute silence. Smiley had long replaced aftershave with deep heat balm, whiffs of the pungent odour invaded their nostrils and their eyes stung. There wasn't a car, a pigeon, cat or a person anywhere about and so they sneakily entered. Smiley they knew, was somewhere inside; he would never leave his material possessions behind.

Alaric led the way up the wooden stairs and just froze, his body flooded in the bright lightning as it tore its way through the house. He ducked low and his foot slipped. Diara pushed on him and he shifted up a bit. When she poked her head pass Alaric, through the gap, her eyes couldn't understand it for a second, it was like some inexplicable vision. But then it hit her, the top of old Smiley's house was gone! Totally torn off! They inched forward and then in the middle of the room their eyes shockingly collided. Then flickered and stared at Smiley's decapitated body lying prostrate on the drenched floor! A closer look revealed that it was sliced by one of the fallen rafters from the lightning shattered roof. Then, as if on cue, tumultuous claps of thunder reigned down from above like a sick, and deafening applause.

Episode Two

Some may call it a fool's theory but Alaric felt that the only sure way to escape from anything is to go in a storm. This brother and sister had to break free from confinement and control of the life they had been imprisoned in. As the terrorising rain began to howl and batter the concrete breeze blocks of old Smiley's once prominent house, they made a hasty retreat.

The coconut trees were being sliced apart and beach huts were being dodged as the wind lifted them like pages ripped from a book. In all this death-defying carnage their hearts knew no fear; their souls had been solidified for these immortal hours.

Mr. Ells was to be their next stop as they ran through a maze of houses that seemed to shriek and ache under the heavy shackles from being boarded up. Their legs hurled and jerked down the winding side streets as the sky rumbled, and heavy rain bounced off the cracked oiled stained roads. As this storm choked the sun, greying the world around them, it symbolised the world's view this twin lived under. They were stifled by prejudice and inflexible judgemental views that were not founded on rational facts or experience about others.

The rain beat against their skin like hammers, it was actually like the arrogance of the world's injustice, harsh and imposing. Alaric's feet were caked in mud and the storm had battered Diara's braided hair into a dripping mess. She wasn't scared, Mr. Ells' number had now been called. Tonight, with this furious storm bearing down on the island, everyone's tense, nervous and in some type of shelter. For some it is a convincing trust to ride out the storm with their strong religious beliefs. Mr. Ells' beliefs didn't seem to transpire to treating others like fellow human beings. His opinions allowed for distinctions that somehow there is a dominant race which excludes others that are not the same. Mr Ells just didn't understand that differences in people are what make us all special and the similarities are what make us human.

Alaric knew that Mr. Ells was an expatriate gentleman of high standing. He was also a Santa Claus face old bastard. His white glistening encircling beard and expensive suits, created a persona of the privileged elite. He wheeled the deals and called the shots, most of all he was looked up to. There was no mistake about his lack of skin colour. Glistening white shone on his face and his money sparkled in this place.

Fine cars, luxurious properties, even the beaches bore his name. His initials were inscribed in the white shinning sands where no blacks were ever allowed to walk through. That beach belonged to Mr Ells.

He never gave them a job in anyone of his numerous financial investment cauldrons which was stirred for him by all his loyal island workers. Mr Ells treated them like criminals; guilty of the one crime all non-whites are guilty of and that was breathing! Mr Ells had told them that his work force didn't need ideas. In his employment there were only two ways of doing things; his way or the wrong way.

Mr Ells once read Alaric's and Diara's qualifications, then he repeatedly said that he knew what his business required and high worker knowledge inhibited productivity, too much education was dangerous. 'Any too qualified 'coloureds' tend to promote trouble.' He had said. Hiring them, he claimed to empathised; he understood their position; he knew what it was like to try to get by but it would be a staff distraction, he deeply clarified.

'Why, workers would waste lots of time just staring at your skin.' Mr Ells had clearly explained. Alaric and Diara had openly questioned some of his abhorrent worker practices and this didn't go down well with Ells.

So, he had summed up his low view on this twin. 'You two are trouble makers.' Then, he had gone on to say, that on the island, 'my workers did as they were told, they didn't question, no fancy rules here on parity, no problems in this place.' Mr Ells had loudly exclaimed, in Alaric and Diara's faces as he angrily pushed them away.

'Why can't you two do like all the others? Do as you are told?' Mr Ells had emphatically shouted at them. Then he warned, that they would be charged for trespassing if they dared returned to his business place. 'Encouraging them to think about forming unions! Where the hell do you two think this place is?' Mr Ells had finally angrily fumed. So, the workers soon kept their distance from Alaric and Diara, if they were to keep their jobs.

Diara pondered a while about Mr Ells, and in particular, the worldwide indignity of the Black race but then she wondered why seek sympathy? Why not demand dignity by rising and prospering? Then she wondered how do you prosper without the right opportunities being opened to you? How do you get in when doors are locked and chained from your entry and only a selected few have the keys? How do you pass over the bridge when sometimes even your own people connive and block you? She loudly sighed and Alaric turned to look at her. With despair set in their eyes this troubled pair rushed on.

The winds cruelly shoved them as the water-swollen roads burst at the seams. The tarmac split, cracked and dropped into gaping holes. This didn't stop them and in no time, they reached Mr Ells' expensive beach-side house. They snaked to the door. Diara hovered at the threshold as more thunderous booms filled the air. The door was already partly opened. Alaric made an obsolete knock as his eyes shifted about. His eyes instantly caught sight of Mr Ells' peg board. Ells' entire life it would seem, was pinned on this peg board but the angry wind stripped the white pieces of paper and scattered them away.

No-one but the already departed could fail to notice the high wave that instantly washed up inside the house! Alaric and Diara jumped back from the rush of water and clutched their weapons. Their eyes bulged from the sockets as a towering wave crashed up and swept Mr Ells right away! Right out to sea, his white, limp, lifeless body laid, floating and rolling on the tempestuous angry sea.

Episode Three

Diara and Alaric had swam like fish and escaped the grip of the tidal surge. They had made it to the life guard hut which the strong gush of waves had repositioned from its beach spot to the centre of the town. Callously tossed upon a town monument splitting it into half. A grand now broken memorial of a reputed white hero who charged great prices for his human non-white, legally owned cargo.

This brother and sister tag-team were clearly aware that their lives were synonymous with this storm. This disturbance of the astronomical state of the atmosphere and environment, especially affecting its surface, and powerfully implying severe weather. Their lives were like that, weather worn by living the lie of island carefree happiness. Outward observances, opposite to their soul's truth.

Like this storm, which created noticeable and significant disruptions to normal conditions as adverse weather progresses, their lives had advanced to antagonistic proportions. These were founded on and resulted from, the normal practices in society to dislike and hate others based on skin colour. Rather than accept everyone as people who are both different but identical as human beings.

Both Alaric and Diara's minds were switching modes, from storms of life to this physical storm. They clearly recognized that storms had the potential to harm lives and property and now they were seeing it first-hand. But this was what they had yearned and prayed for; this golden opportunity to get their own back. They clung onto the window ledge of the hut as the road was completely flooded and the water was still rapidly rising.

Surprisingly, they were still in possession of their weapons. The straps of these were still tied to their wrists like manacled reminders of this night's mission as they pressed on. Alaric kicked the swirling filthy water and smiled at Diara. He was maintaining a cool detachment to his targets. At this moment, he preferred not to think of them, only the harsh words or sinister looks which they gave them but when he did, it was as if they were already dead.

He thought of them as meeting their destiny the hidden power believed to control future events. Fate, that tiny word and he was merely the channel. Everyone must die sometime, and he considered it a good way to go. No illness, no drawn-out goodbyes. They would be just waiting out the storm, anxiously hoping for it to pass. Oblivious one second and gone the next. Simple. Plain. Uncomplicated. Convenient. Painless! Probably but no, it should be excruciating. He didn't care. Diara nudged him, and pointed with her chin in the direction of their next target.

Sonny Boy got the short straw, this was his turn to dance with the devil. They weren't so sure who Sonny Boy really was. His soft curly hair, very lightish skin made him hang on above the lowest rung of the island's expatriate approval ladder. He once said to Alaric and Diara, 'Asians have culture but West Indians have problems.' They were still trying to figure that statement out.

Strangely enough, Sonny Boy had always maintained that he was their friend but they soon learnt that he was a two-faced, lying, back-stabbing, cunt of a man if ever there was one. He smiled with them and came around when 'gran gran' cooked the meals which he loved; these were free. Sonny Boy went to school in August and he was not Scottish but he was a brilliant conman; he roped them into working with him on a building project but took the biggest cut. Alaric and Diara quickly grasped that to get level with a snake, you must crawl on the ground so they weren't caught in that way again but were seized in others, by this excuse for occupying living space, called Sonny Boy.

This brother and sister promptly discovered that Sonny boy was one of those people who showered when dressed; there was a short cut and easy way out for everything. The space in Sonny Boy's head was unoccupied, no goodness resided inside. The content of his greed gave the signs. He pedalled the illegal skin whitening creams which he guaranteed would definitely please. At a price which was heavily paid by those who dared to try, to change their race. Sonny Boy had said that in the absence of privilege of the right skin colour to get by, then try to even the odds by lightening the face to sneak in on the side. He saw nothing wrong with subterfuge and counterfeit pride, once his creams' sales were high.

Sonny Boy staunchly believed in nonvoluntary wealth distribution and so he glibly stole from them. His dastardly deeds were inexcusable. He learnt their weaknesses and their strengths and then used these against them. This was a toxic relationship, one which they just couldn't shake as they got small jobs through him.

Behind their backs he was known to speak disparagingly about their colour status. He joked and laughed, mocking them with derisive comments and excluding them from his home barbeques and get togethers. At these times they just weren't, well, really friends, as Sonny Boy's excuses went, 'Ah only had a few very, very close, close friends, don't worry, next time it will be a bigger do, one that you two can come to. It will be a beach time do, with more of your kinda people.' Sonny Boy's pretexts replayed in their heads. This now was Sonny Boy's day; his time to face the emergency moral and social justice call.

Waist high and wading through the increasingly deep, slimy water with the relentless torrents of rain pounding down, seemed merciless. But payback was such a great wage earned through hurt, pain, deceit, slights and most of all exclusion from real life.

Alaric had relived this day in his mind over and again. He dreamt of his machete connecting to the flesh, soft and chubby, and making a satisfying squish as the sharp stainless-steel blade descended deep enough to make his victim scream. He swung the machete in his hand, raising the blade above his head all the while delving and chopping deeper and deeper! The skin was gashing to pieces as the machete struck, the sound of muscles and tissues being gouged and shards of skin flying everywhere with blood splashing and spouting filled the air. Then, the final mighty blow would break the sound barrier with the excruciating screams of those who had come to feel helpless and passive in the face of his steel! The cry was a vivid, penetrating sound, throaty chokes mixed with an tormented roar. He smirked, and snatched the machete away from the now dying soul.

The quivering body, juddering and trembling like a headless chicken with the profuse blood flowing freely from the deep holes. The torrent of the life spring spurt out in all directions, red fluid gushing up all over him. He turned away as the trembling stopped. The bitter sweet trace of blood stinging on his skin; the skin of rejection, the skin of defeat. The skin which just couldn't make him complete.

As a cold tear fell, Diara noticed and she gently wiped it away. His murderous thought revelry now abruptly stopped. Their breast strokes resumed, then sharply ceased, they brought them to what was once the town hang out spot for all the drunks, gamblers and touts. It was now completely flattened and its galvanised roof had become a sailing raft for the sober and the drunk, if they had the capacity to climb aboard and stay afloat.

Was this good luck or misfortune that Sonny Boy was now the sole survivor clinging onto this makeshift life raft? His impassioned cries could be heard for miles. As the raft was channelled towards Alaric and Diara, Sonny Boy's eyes were filled with dread. His head bobbed about and he screeched like an angry parrot whose wings had been clipped. Within his inaudible babble, Alaric could only make out the words, "Ah can't swim! Ah can't swim! Ah can't swim!" Jumping out from Sonny Boy's wide and terrified opened mouth!

The howling wind was speedily blowing, not only the raft but his trembling, petrified voice far away! Diara and Alaric rushed towards the raft, primed their positions with weapons prepared for swift delivery of this end of life game.

The raft's direction was rapidly changing as the flood waters raced so did Alaric and Diara. Sonny Boy clutched and grabbed the raft tighter and tighter. By now his frantic fingers were clutching and scratching at everything and nothing. Soon they were entwined with the metal TV aerial that was still attached to the roof, come life raft.

Then instantly, the sky lit up with brilliant white hues. As sharp streaks of lightning blazed down from the sky above, a mighty lightning bolt instantly set Sonny Boy's hand alight! His body violently shook as his heart's electrical rhythm plunged into cardiac arrest! Alaric and Diara quickly waded, splashed and paddled over to the raft. Their eyes popped out and could undoubtedly see, that Sonny Boy, was surely, as dead, as he ever could be!

Episode Four

Looking around in the despairing motion of the rising waters, catching their breaths and breathing deep, they watched as more houses began to be tested, by this ferocious storm. The roofs, the windows, the walls, bore the weight of this storm's rage. Roofs flapped, the single panes of glass clattered in their aging frames, not even the walls stood secure.

Most of these houses Diara and Alaric recognized were built by those artisans whom worked with the now, late Sonny Boy. So, what could be expected to happen to them? Exactly what was truly occurring; weakly built, easily destroyed. Just like how their lives were built, engineered by the human architects of foul deceit who cut them apart day by day with their vile classification of man, based on their imposed skin colour scales, 'White over Brown over Black' and this was a certain inhuman organization which broke, sliced, cut and demeaned.

Alaric and Diara's thoughts, like this pounding rain, tumbled further back. The brown-skinned mulatto, oh how they hated that word! One born from the Portuguese and Spanish fifteenth century word 'mula' which meant mule. The offspring of a donkey and a horse.

This was the referencing used for persons who had one descended White European and one Black African descended parent. Their parents, loved each other; neither was a donkey nor horse and none of their children were mules! Alaric and Diara knew that these big ass-cat name callers really had shit for brains!

Breaking these thoughts, the wind screamed louder around each dwelling as if enraged it should exist, pushing its way under every door, breaking it open to extinguish the lives trapped inside. This fierce storm represented white arrogance and pride, as how it tore at their souls and aggressively diced them apart.

Diara and Alaric swam onwards they neared the imposing church. It was built on a hilltop and was literally 'a shelter in the times of storms,' not just a reference to part of a hymn. The church was packed with frightened souls in search of sanctuary but also in a desperate and urgent quest for redemption for their mortal souls. The non-blacks huddled up on the altar with their expensive raincoats, and precious possessions while all the others were below. No one said their prayers out loud, they just bunched together and pleaded for 'His' protection, a blessed book gripped tight.

Diara and Alaric peeped inside and then moved back to the side of the church. Their search was not for refuge nor safety from pursuit of danger from this horrific storm. It was for Father Chadler, the spiritual defender of this island. This troubled pair had Father Chadler high on their list. He was the one they would settle the last score with. He was the one that would be under the moral microscope to answer the questions for His God who moved in mysterious ways.

Father Chadler had come out to the island from his homeland Britain. He had said that he used to be in the army and had told them to take some concrete pills and hardened up! Alaric and Diara felt that he must have meant the Salvation Army; there was no way he was a soldier who defended any cause. Father Chadler championed the philosophy of constructive ambiguity. He took no stance for them in their trials. He remained a passive observer, with non-committal responses when they were being put down by others.

'It's not that bad, people have different views and you two are over sensitive, God will take care of you.' Father Chadler would try to convince them that God would clean up man's mess when he knew that God gave all humans free choice in the way they behaved with others.

Alaric and Diara undoubtedly understood that Father Chadler belonged to the sitting on the fence alliance. He never wanted to understand that if every day in their lives, they were constantly beaten, then their scars would never really heal.

Consequently, any slight, brush, touch against that battered skin made it agonizingly painful with tremendous hurt. This is the way that ugly racism worked. Their skin was highly bruised and charged!

Father Chadler didn't want to recognize reality; he wanted a happily ever after fairy tale. Despite their obvious hurt and pain, they were to join Father Chadler's church; sit behind the same people, who half-smiled with them on a Sunday and frowned at them the remainder of the week because they just weren't the right skin colour.

Then there was the choir which their voices could be added to, he had told them and this would certainly help them build self-esteem. Alaric and Diara thought that many people in his choir had to have, led extremely reckless lives to have been able to sing so low. Like this choir, every step in Alaric and Diara's lives was a low chord of disdain. A cord which became a yoke around their necks for being guilty of the skin they inhabited. Father Chadler had to be interrogated, his end could not be swift.

This pair wanted some answers as to why a great big mighty God allowed so much hopelessness to enter their lives and bring them to this point of no return; a moral cul de sac. What was wrong with this big great mighty God? Was he too in need of some serious therapy? Or was he a racist too? But, then, didn't he make us all the same? Alaric and Diara contemplated more.

Why was life so unfair towards skin colour? Why did the world believe that innate racial differences exist? There is no distinction if black and white DNA is examined separately without identification.

This twin contemplated, and just could not understand the world-wide view surrounding race and class alongside the terrible abuse which the so-called respectable humans dished out.

The questions kept punching their brains like the water torrents and the turbulent gales. If one race is superior over the others, then why do people from all races die? Why is the superior race not immortal? Why can't those of the superior race live forever? Why do all races get terminal illness? Why do all races sit on the toilet? Why do we breathe the same oxygen? Surely, those in the superior race deserve better air!

Alaric and Diara's brains were raging hot fires! They knew that racial superiority was just a great fantasy! More and more questions spew from their minds. What is it that promotes hate and demeaning racial attitudes? Why can't hate be replaced with love? Like the powerful lightning, this twin's feelings flashed on and on. This state of affairs, skin colour rage and resentment had savaged their identity and in turn, it had now turned them into savages!

This twin summed up their thoughts and were brought out of the abys of their feelings, as the lightning increased its severity and brutally struck a tall tree toppling it from its position, barely missing the church. This sent branches sprawling across the flooded road, as the churning waters stripped the leaves.

Alaric and Diara hid their weapons behind their backs and scuttled to the rear of the church. They were certain that Father Chadler lived in the manse just behind the church. In an instant they reached the house, the door was wide open. Diara and Alaric could see that Father Chadler was kneeling in prayer with his back to the doorway. They looked at each other and smirked, 'some really easy prey,' they thought.

They inched closer and closer. This was as good a time as any to send him to his maker without the pain of interrogation. They had lived with so many unanswered questions before so what was the point of waiting for useless answers anyway? 'Yes! Yes! Just do it!' Their brains screamed!

They could have the delight of inflicting the mortal wounds, they both thought, without him even seeing them coming. Alaric and Diara knew that this stormy night was designed for murder, all the dead from storms are assumed to have been the victims of the storm. On small islands no one bothers about post mortems, too many bodies, too much decomposition! Too little money. Who gives a damn? Killed by the storm! This would be the belief.

They looked at Father Chadler once more. That's it! They decided. He deserved it! Let's do it! He must get it! Just as their feet hit the doormat a ferocious wind blew and an oversized book with extra-large print fell from a corner shelf and completely blocked their path.

They both looked down at the bold huge words of the exposed page. The words were those of Fanny Crosby's, Hymn (1869), 'Rescue the perishing, care for the dying, snatch them in pity from sin and the grave; weep o'er the erring one, lift the fallen, tell them of Jesus the mighty to save...(Hymnary.org,-Public Domain) Right now, at this moment in time, Alaric and Diara certainly didn't have salvation as a consideration on their minds. The hurt and pain of bigotry had brought them to this point. This brother and sister raised their darkened eyes from the page. They gazed heavenwards and then menacingly lowered their eyes towards Father Chadler. The machete and hatchet angrily dangled from their hands as a thunderous boom resounded while Bob Marley's 'War' resounded in their heads.

Visit YouTube and listen:

https://www.youtube.com/watch?v=XXxEilzNJcE

Epilogue

Who gets to be happy? Globally, conscious and unconscious bias surrounding the life actions of all people determine the answer to this question. A starting and reference point should focus on the understanding that rrespect for others and their differences can never be legalized. To break the negative cycle of racism, from very early, encouraging positive attitudes in young children about diversity, is critical to developing well balanced adults who have no race hate.

Furthermore, men engage in superficial talk of building bridges between races; often designed for advancing some type of hidden agenda. These men are the owners of the bridge building materials, and are the engineers who also own the explosives which covertly blow them up as soon as any type of façade of social and moral construction commences towards positive race relations. No one race holds the title deeds to this planet; therefore, every race is entitled to peaceful enjoyment of this earth to live without fear of being who you are. May we all share it in respect, peace and love for all people irrespective of sin colour, gender, sexual orientation, ability or disability.

About the Author

Alexis V

Inspired by the often exciting highly imaginative conversations, sharp witted and entertaining anecdotes of the teenage students whom she educated during a long professional teaching career which included varying educational leadership posts, Alexis V turned her penmanship from marking assignments to a more electrifying pursuit, fiction writing and more recently concept children's books for SEN.

Alexis V writes from her study while overlooking a beautiful green tree-lined field which supports her creative thought. Originally from Barbados, she lives in Suffolk, UK, is married and has two adult daughters. She enjoys cooking, reading and riding a tandem bicycle with her husband, who obviously sits at the front!

Other Books by this Author

Engulfing Events is a series of three crime fiction novels, written by Alexis V. The series has a multi-cultural setting within South America and the Caribbean, and follows the young characters, Erica Durr, Ethan Miller, Sofia Grant and Carlos Carrillo as they battle through a mine field of unsolicited trouble and dangerous life shaking encounters.

The novels in this trilogy are titled, Girl Arrested release date 2015, Child Taken, 2016 and Fear Undetermined, 2018. Each novel although part of a series, is its own standalone story; with a complete climax within the book. You don't need to read the next novel to get to the ending but if you do, you are guaranteed not to be disappointed.

A troubled and unhappy home life leads young Erica into a secret relationship with an older man. She meets with her lover but later wakes to find herself covered in blood on board her father's yacht and the prime suspect in a murder scene. Luckily, she has two allies in the form of best friend Sophia and new neighbour Ethan, who over the course of the next few days move heaven and earth to help her clear her name. As they investigate, they become immersed in the dark and dangerous world of the illegal gold trade and people trafficking.

Warm tropical waters, idyllic shores, a paradise in the distance; a Caribbean cruise never to be forgotten. Lurking amidst the calm seas is an evil force; unleashing the never ending nightmare when a child is taken! With forty-eight hours to find her, the gates of agony are thrown wide open. The parents and their friends go through hell on earth to save her! They must fight their way past labyrinths and a host of deadly enemies if they are to rescue the child and hold together the family's enduring love and trust.

A wonderful night goes all wrong and lives are thrown into peril when a young pilot is feared to be either violently killed or abducted from his bachelor night pre-wedding party. His name is smeared by being subsequently accused of attempting to kill his rich father and suspected of staging his own disappearance. His fiancée and two best friends must find out what happened to him before it is too late. There is one problem, the trail leads them to one of the most dangerous and deadly places on earth, the Amazon.

Suddenly caught up in deep trouble not of their own making, four young work colleagues find themselves thrown into an intelligent and elaborate operation of an organized plot to bring London to its knees. The trouble which they were in seemed beyond their capabilities, horrifically blood curdling, sinister and death inducing. Being in trouble was just way bigger than any iceberg, as their wits are tested and lives are cold-bloodedly taken. Getting in was easy, but can they get out.

Rebekah Fuller's main encouragement through her limiting teenage years was her friendship with Annabelle Foster, a pretty and popular girl. The two girls meet the boys of each other's dreams but still managed to fall deeply in love, at a time when war is declared and lives are hurled into uncertainty and confusion! The war and Rebekah's mother's excessive tendency to overprotect, sweeps her into a minefield of uncharted pitfalls and dramatic life changes. These dynamics, not only determine Rebekah's future but her passions, her pains, her hopes and dreams. They lead her to several emotional valleys but would she manage to finally reach love's mountain top?

How do you imagine your future? Imagining the future helps us to prepare for problems and be more equipped to solve them but what if your entire future was totally and absolutely within the hands of the State? A State which was based on scoring and your ability for happiness, success and health, rested in those ratings. What would you do? Would you contemplate to leave or to remain? This mini-story is a funny view of things which may possibly come to pass; with hidden truths but powerful meanings!

For many, counterfeit love can masquerade as genuine affection, through manipulation and control. Occurring often during young years, from not wanting to be left out from life's constants and reinforced by great sex. All these fuel a bad bond leading to relationship entrapment. Options for getting out and starting over, appear elusive and emotional walls crumble. Life becomes buried beneath regret and the cycle of hopelessness spins. This short story is a glimpse of the life of a young woman which exposes these relationship issues. Can she find the strength to get out?

A splendid inspirational keepsake, which is an ideal gift for family and friends of any special, loved one. It's filled with heartwarming sentiments, a page with blank lines to insert a personalized recipient's and sender's details. Suitable for a daughter, sister, mother, friend or any woman who has touched the lives of others and has 'passed on' but whose life remains as 'Enduring Memories.'

One young woman's view of her struggle to reveal her true 'identity' to her Caribbean heritage parents and extended family. She clearly understood the torment which ensued for many people to reconcile and understand that she was an individual, unique and with specific differences. She knew that there would be an outpouring of support for her if perhaps she had a terminal illness but there were explicit and understood principles governing and surrounding her 'difference' and often within the Caribbean there was little mercy.

Is your child a 'runner,' or perhaps one who is autistic with Special Education Needs? Then this book can provide support for helping the child who frequently runs off to understand when it is safe to run and when it is dangerous to do so. The young child and in particular the autistic child, often does not have real awareness of dangers in their environment. This book can provide support to your child in developing safety awareness.

In adolescent years, teenagers can make judgments and decisions on their own but most often in situations where they have time to think. On the other hand, when they have to make quick decisions or in social situations, their choices are often influenced by external elements like the peer group. Read to find out about the different types of choices teenagers face. See if Gordon can resist pressure from others and as a teenager, can you?

Understanding, colour, shape and size are essentials which children need to know in order to master Reading, Writing, Language and Math. It is a tool for learning many skills in all subject areas. For autistic children who are mostly visual thinkers and learners, color, shape and size can be used to create learning steps, helping them to pick up words and concepts, and develop basic skills. Ultimately, the goal is to motivate the child to develop better verbal communication skills. Thomas Reads about Colour, Shape and size, can be used to stimulate awareness of these concepts.

Building friendships can be challenging for any child and especially so for the SEN child who may require additional support as a result of a broad range of needs. These needs may be in regard to emotional and behavioural difficulties, or how the child relates to and behaves with other people. This book is intended to deliberately focus on key social skills to support the child in developing friendships.

Alexis V

Printed in Great Britain
by Amazon